NO MORE LOCUSTS!!!
It's
RESTORATION
Time

By

DONNA R. IDE

*"So I will restore to you the years
that the swarming locust has eaten…"*
Joel 2:25a

Contents

Preface

To be perfectly honest, this whole 'book' thing really scared me. I'd been studying the subject of restoration, through the eyes of Nehemiah, for years, when I became more intrigued and wandered into the book of Joel.

Let me back up. I am not a theologian nor am I a well known seer. Actually, neither am I just plain ole well known. I received Jesus as my Lord back in 1975 while searching for the truth about life outside of the human realm. I was living in a haunted house at the time and wanted to know where these spirits came from so I became very involved in the occult; witchcraft, ESP, Tarot cards, ghost hunting, Ouija boards, etc. At the same time I desperately needed to know the truth about heaven, because life here on earth just was not making it for me. Skimming through all the options, I found myself attending a weekly Bible study. THE Truth was finally becoming real to me and on Easter Sunday, while attending my Episcopalian church service, I silently asked Jesus Christ to take my life over. Rays of Light invaded my being over and over and over again. It made me feel clean on the inside and gave my great peace and joy. I guess you'd call it a radical salvation in that my life has never been the same since that day. 35+ years later and I am still searching, crying out for more of God.

Well, I guess He heard my cry for more of Him because one sunny Sunday afternoon, after I'd come home from church, the Lord's presence filled up my living room. I was sitting at my desk and reading about restoration, from the book of Joel, when the glory of the Lord came in.

His glorious presence was so thick and heavy that I felt as if my head was being pushed down between my shoulders. I fell to my knees and stayed there for what seemed like hours unable to move.

Yup, I was terrified too. It was there, in that position that the Lord spoke to me and told me to gather all my notes on restoration. He then used the 'B' word; BOOK. He said to write a book and title it, *'No More Locusts, It's Restoration Time'*.

At that time in my life, I was involved in a church planting, however, by then most all the responsibilities I previously had, had been taken over as folks stepped up and into their rightful positions, enabling me the time to write a book with very few interruptions.

During those days and nights, the Lord directed me to the accounts, in the Old Testament, that described the building of King Solomon's Temple. Many times His glory would fill up my living room as I'd read about the Temple made with hands. There were times when I was taken up and brought into Solomon's Temple. I saw the gold that lined the walls. I smelled the fragrance of incense. I felt the heavy glory cloud and heard the beautiful, continuous worship. It was a perfect place. He would speak to me and say, "Do you see My glory?" "Can you see the beauty I've afforded this place for My people?" "Listen to the worship. Listen to the one sound." I saw the glory of God fly back and forth, as an electric current, that hit the walls ladened with gold and sending LIFE everywhere. It was magnificent! I spent my days transcribing what I heard and saw. Soon *'No More Locusts, It's Restoration Time'* was birthed.

I have told very few of this experience. However, now I have written my experience to encourage you. Beloved, it's restoration time!

During the meetings with the Lord, He revealed nine attributes that are being restored to the Body of Christ, His Living Temple, in these last days.

They are Beauty, Covenant, Wealth, Joy, Unity, Worship, Glory, Wisdom and Government.

As you read about these, PLEASE, take them for yourself as Father God personally imparts His very essence to you.

Allow His glory to invade your space and restore the years the enemy has stolen.

Introduction

The Farm Story

The weather was raw and gusty, the weekend we moved, as the sun peeked in and out of the gray November clouds. Our dream of owning a farm had finally come true. The 'farm' consisted of a seven room, one hundred year old Victorian farmhouse that had been vacant for years and was in need of much TLC; a three car garage with its sagging roof, minus the center beam and garage doors; the barn, that was attached to the garage, which was large enough to hold a half dozen or so barnyard animals; and the greenhouse, which had been vandalized by the neighborhood kids, not one pane left unbroken. The chicken coop consisted of some old boards thrown together and hammered to the side of the barn. Along with the property came the weirdest group of chickens. They were all sizes, colors and shapes and not too productive with the eggs. What a motley crew! And yes, Toby, the barnyard dog had been terribly neglected and suffered from malnutrition. At first glance, all we saw was a place we could call 'our own farm', yet in reality, it was a major work of restoration that only time and a crowbar would disclose.

We started on the house first. Patience had its perfect work as we scraped off years and layers of wallpaper, uncovering more work that revealed cracked walls and horsehair plaster. As we dug a little deeper, prodding the walls, outdated wiring was just waiting to be replaced. Everyday proved to be a new adventure in restoration. It seemed no matter what area of the house or garage or barn or greenhouse we worked on, a project would surface that only tender loving care and much 'elbow grease' would make perfect and beautiful.

As days turned into weeks and weeks into months, the fragile resemblance of 'a farm' finally became a reality. The worn, rotten wood, in the barn, was replaced with new weather treated planking. Where there was no center beam in the garage, a huge, strong one was put in place, enabling its frame to, once again, stand straight and tall, no more sagging. The greenhouse glass was replaced by being meticulously caulked and pointed. The chickens' shack was torn off the barn and replaced with a real chicken coop, perches and all. Even the old hens were 'put out to pasture' and a fresh flock of Rhode Island Reds was welcomed, with eggs abounding. Toby, the barnyard collie, received much food and love and a good grooming.

The house was finally a home! Restoration on this structure not only included new wiring but also new plumbing, and ornate Victorian hardware. Doors and frames replaced the old broken ones, and hardwood floors were refinished, revealing beautiful oak planking. Finally, fresh paint and vintage designed wallpaper were added to complete the restoration project.

Was it worth all the hard work, long hours and sacrificed vacations to get the place restored? Yes, without a doubt, because anything less would have been a tragedy in work and time. We knew that if anything had been left half finished, in time it would have weakened and destroyed the new, doubling the cost. Moreover, the tangible love and care that was endlessly displayed far surpassed the work and value of the finished product.

Moral of the Story

If that old farmhouse had had a voice during those days of restoration it would have screamed, "OUCH, THAT HURTS!" many times with groanings and curse words highlighting the process. It would have said, "What are you taking my wiring out for? It still works!" However, it was obsolete and could have been dangerous. Restoration is not always fun. The thing about restoration is that the hardest, most challenging work, the work that takes the longest, is hidden from view when the project is finished. The surface is only a façade. Its true value, its most costly work, is covered and protected from harm.

Jesus summed it up well when as He spoke these parables, in **Luke 5:36-39**:

36 "No one puts a piece from a new garment on an old one; otherwise the new makes a tear, and also the piece that was taken out of the new does not match the old.

37 "And no one puts new wine into old wineskins; or else the new wine will burst the wineskins and be spilled, and the wineskins will be ruined.

38 "But new wine must be put into new wineskins, and both are preserved.

39 "And no one, having drunk old wine, immediately desires new; for he says, 'The old is better.'"

Just like an old garment or a used wineskin, or an old farmhouse, our 'house', our very being, where the Holy Spirit takes up residence, our temple must be made ready for this grand finale of God. We must allow the Holy Spirit to shed His exposing Light on ALL the old hidden useless, stuff, without protesting and saying, 'the old is better'. Strongholds, like dead rotten wood, that have been keeping us from growing and advancing, must be pulled up. Time that leads to nothing, in our daily routine, has a way of stealing our day if it is used via the dictates of the world's time clock and not the Lord's. It will be wasted and then lost if it is not sanctified in the Blood of Jesus. However, we have a promise in **Psalm 31:15** that say, *My times are in Your hands.*

We must allow the Spirit of God to be honest with us. He is the Comforter, not the Accuser. For once, we must allow Him to expose hidden agendas and plans not made of God that we may have been nurturing for years. It's time to let go and at last give it over to the Lord and allow Him to be the Judge and the Restorer. We must ask, "Is this really of You, Lord, or do I need to let go of it, as a dead work and get on with the rest of my life?" He'll let you know. Be honest with Him, He loves you and wants the best for you.

Just like the old farmhouse, we must pull out all the old worn, rotten 'wood'; i.e., the attitudes, character traits, and wrong thinking, that just don't line up with God's Word and allow Him to work within. After all, He is the Master Carpenter!

What a restoration job He will do! Glory!

Chapter One

Restoration to Usher in End Time Harvest

So much has been said about revival past, present and future. History has been earmarked by great moves of the Holy Spirit resulting in holiness thus bringing the most hardened heart to repentance. Listen now, to the cry of the church, as of old; "Send revival, Lord! Pour out Your Spirit in this dry land!" All around the globe the Church is in birth pangs waiting for the sons of men to be revealed. Most believers would agree that this is to be THE Last Revival–THE LAST ONE! There is no going back for another try. We are living in the last of the last times. Is the church ready for this great harvest? What needs to be done to usher in this mighty move of God? The author of the book of Acts says it well, ... *and that He may send Jesus Christ, who was preached to you before, whom heaven must receive until the <u>times</u> of <u>restoration</u>*

of all things, which God has spoken by the mouth of all His holy prophets since the world began. **Acts 3:20-21**

Strong's Concordance Definition:

Restoration/Restitution 605 (from 600) Reconstitution Restoration: **a.** of a true theocracy; **b.** of the perfect state before the fall. 600 – To reconstitute (in health, home or organization); restore again to place down permanently.

Times – 5550–A space in time, a fixed or special occasion, season

According to these verses, Jesus is being held in heaven until the **times**, the 'space in time', the 'fixed or special occasion', of the 'season' of **restoration** comes to the church, the time when ALL THINGS will be restored, reconstituted in our health, our homes, and our organizations. And with this 'special occasion' comes the awesome responsibility of adhering and submitting to His promises as THE Living Word of God.

BE GLORIFIED O LORD, MOST HIGH!

Let us hear what one of His holy prophets, Joel, has to say about this 'space in time' this 'special occasion'

25 "So I will <u>restore</u> to you the years that the swarming locust has eaten, the crawling locust, the consuming locust, and the chewing locust, My great army which I sent among you.

26 You shall eat in plenty and be satisfied, and praise the name of the Lord your God, Who has dealt wondrously with you; and My people shall never be put to shame.

27 Then you shall know that I am in the midst of Israel, and that I am the Lord your God and there is no other. My people shall never be put to shame.

28a And it shall come to pass, afterward, that I will pour out My Spirit on all flesh;" **Joel 2:25-28a**

These verses enlighten, magnify, and enhance Acts 3:20-21. The timeline has been set. We also see the order of restoration and revival through both scriptures as they dovetail together, bringing in the fullness of what God has in store for the Body of Christ these last days.

Strong's Concordance Definition:

<u>Restore</u> – 7999 – To be in a <u>covenant of peace</u>; to be safe (in mind, body, or estate); to be completed; to reciprocate; make amends; make an end, finish, full, give again, make good, repay, make to be at peace, make

prosperous, requite, make restitution, reward, by impli-
cation to be friendly.

This definition enlarges our expectation of what the
Lord God Almighty has for us during this 'space in time',
this 'special occasion'. Joel goes on to prophesy about a
time when we will **eat in plenty, and be satisfied. He
will deal wondrously with us, and we will NEVER be
put to shame**!

Blessings upon blessings upon blessings FIRST, and
then REVIVAL.

*And it shall come to pass, AFTERWARD, that I will
pour out My Spirit on all flesh...* **(Joel 2:28a)**

So, What is it That God Wants to Restore?

*19 "Repent therefore and be converted, that your sins
may be blotted out, so that times of refreshing may come
from the presence of the Lord,"* **Acts 3:19**
*14 "If My people who are called by My name will
humble themselves, and pray and seek My face, and
turn from their wicked ways, then I will hear from
heaven, and will forgive their sin and heal their land."*
II Chronicles 7:14

What do these two scriptures have in common?
Both are calling for a move of God. Both are requiring

repentance and sanctification time as a continual life-style of holiness. In II Chronicles, God is speaking to Solomon at the completion of the temple. In Acts, God is speaking to those who are to be converted and become a part of the Living Temple. Both scriptures speak of a temple; the Old Testament, the Temple made of stone, the Most Holy Place; the New Testament, the Living Temple, made of flesh, where the Holy Spirit resides.

God spoke in II Chronicles 7:14 to Solomon in the night hours, on the very day he had dedicated the most beautiful 'holding place' ever created for God's presence. Solomon gathered all the people that day, to usher in the Shekinah presence of our Lord. He had prayed. After a time of sacrifice, praise, and thanksgiving, he asked God to come and stamp His approval on the temple. God did. His glory and fire fell, and consumed the sacrifice, causing the people to fall on their faces in worship. God came to Solomon that night and he said that if His people humble themselves, pray, seek His FACE, not hand, turn (repent) from their wicked ways, and completely sell out for Him, then He would forgive and heal their land. Solomon built the temple, God came to dwell and intended to never leave. **II Chronicles 7:16** says, *"For now I have chosen and sanctified this house, that My name may be there forever; and My eyes and My heart will be there perpetually."*

We have a record, in the building and completion of Solomon's temple, of a perfect place and time when His temple was created for His Chosen to usher in His presence, to reside perpetually, on earth. It was perfect!

Let us take a closer look at this time and this temple, this Most Holy Place and use it as a comparison and a blueprint of how God is working to restore the Living Temple, the one made without walls.

Webster's Definition: <u>Restore</u>

1. To give back something taken away, lost
2. To bring back to a former or normal condition
3. To put a person back in a place, position, rank, etc.
4. To bring back to health, strength
5. To reestablish something which has passed away, as a custom, system of government

With these scriptures and definitions in mind, let us look at nine attributes, values, that the Lord deposited in Solomon's temple. Comprehend the greatness afforded to us, His Living Temple, as Father God brings to pass to His beloved Body of Christ the *"...times of restoration of all things..."*.

Chapter Two

9 Attributes From King Solomon's Temple

(A Perfect Blueprint to Restore the Living Temple)

L ook at nine attributes, from King Solomon's temple, and take some time to read and meditate on each scripture passage as they come alive to paint a picture of God's majestic plan to impart these values into His Living Temple.

Attribute #1
God's Perfect <u>Beauty</u> to be Restored

6a And he decorated the house with precious stones for beauty…

7 He also overlaid the house—the beams and door-posts, its walls and doors—with gold; and he carved cherubim on the walls.

8 And he made the Most Holy Place. ...He overlaid it with six hundred talents of fine gold. ($3,456,000,000)

9 The weight of the nails was fifty shekels of gold; and he overlaid the upper area with gold. (note:$96,000 worth of nails!)

14 And he made the veil of blue and purple and crimson and fine linen, and wove cherubim into it.

II Chronicles 3:6a-9, 14

12 "Concerning this temple which you are building, if you walk in My statutes, execute My judgments, keep all My commandments, and walk in them, then I will perform My word with you, which I spoke to your father David."

13 "And I will dwell among the children of Israel, and will not forsake My people Israel."

14 So Solomon built the temple and finished it.

18 The inside of the temple was cedar, carved with ornamental buds and open flowers. All was cedar; there was no stone to be seen.

20b He overlaid it (the inner sanctuary) with pure gold, and overlaid the altar of cedar.

21 So Solomon overlaid the inside of the temple with pure gold. He stretched gold chains across the front of the inner sanctuary; and he overlaid it with gold.

22 The whole temple he overlaid with gold, until he had finished all the temple; also he overlaid with gold the entire altar that was by the inner sanctuary.

28 Also he overlaid the cherubim with gold.
I Kings 6:12-14, 18-22, 28

30 And the floor of the temple he overlaid with gold, both the inner and outer sanctuaries.

32 The two doors were of olive wood; and he carved on them figures of cherubim, palm trees, and open flowers, and overlaid them with gold; and he spread gold on the cherubim and on the palm trees.

35 Then he carved cherubim, palm trees, and open flowers on them (two doors), and overlaid them with gold applied evenly on the carved work. **I Kings 6: 30, 32, 35**

Do you see the beauty, and the greatness afforded to God's Most Holy Place, a place to bring Himself into the earth? There was no other place He chose to be at that time, on earth. Indeed, heaven and earth kissed with the completion of His House. Even with the building of this mighty place, unity strengthened, love abounded, and strongholds came down. Solomon knew he only had this to do. This was his sole desire, his aim, his life, at this time of his life. He worked at making this temple so perfect, so beautiful, beyond whatever was before on earth, to bring to pass his father's plan, the plan God gave King David.

Father God put the desire in his heart; He worked Solomon up to the point that even he believed he could do this. The heavenly Father showed him what He wanted; Solomon worked the task into being. He had everything he needed because God gave it to him. He gave him who he was and He also gave King Solomon freewill.

This temple was made by man's hand, yet was designed, directed, and overseen by the Most High God. No idol, no foreign god could function around this place because the Almighty was there, in His fullness.

His people were so excited at the building of the temple. There was 'electricity' in the air the whole time with perfect unity abounding as an adhesive, holding each other together as a perfect bond, making all function as one. Father God became vulnerable to His people and this temple made it so easy for all to realize how they were one with their Creator. His beauty abounded!

11 And it came to pass when the priests came out of the Most Holy Place (for all the priests who were present had sanctified themselves, without keeping to their divisions),

13 indeed it came to pass, when the trumpeters and singers were as one, to make one sound to be heard in praising and thanking the Lord, and when they lifted up their voice with the trumpets and cymbals and instruments of music, and praised the Lord, saying:

"For He is good,

For His mercy endures forever."

that the house, the house of the Lord, was filled with a cloud,

14 so that the priests could not continue ministering because of the cloud; for the glory of the Lord filled the house of God. **II Chronicles 5: 11, 13,14**

There had never been another time, on earth, such as that time. His priests, His king, and His people were all in one accord just for HIM. King Solomon answered the call and submitted to his God, the priests submitted to their God and the prophets heard and obeyed. All was well in His kingdom. This temple was the outward display of how God's people were devoted to their Lord Jehovah.

This Most Holy Place, this house, this temple was adorned with the Father's love, His refined beauty and was sanctified to hold Himself. Do you see this place, this perfect beauty? Can you smell the fragrance coming from within? This aroma traveled throughout the area drawing God's people to worship. Do you hear the voices, as one voice, going up to heaven? The voices of praise and thanksgiving were as thick as thunder to the heavens. No one could stop this spontaneous worship with all being in one accord. The instruments became alive! His anointing became liquid and dripped off the instruments, as oil, the fragrance being God, Himself, undeniably His scent. Know that scent. As the people of Israel walked into the courtyard, their senses became alert and alive. Senses are God given. We are not to be controlled by them, however, we must allow them to be a part of our sanctified lives; sanctified senses. Only the Redeemed know this. He has set so much aside for the Redeemed, as we listen to what He is saying, and believe, and then act with faith to work the plan. Truly, change is happening from within the Body of Christ. The cries for His glory and His beauty and His holiness to be heard and seen are manifesting today.

Solomon followed through with the course that was set before him. His father David cut the way for his son, and God ordained it. If Solomon had finished his time with the same fervor, innocence, and holiness that he started with, as king, history would have been different. God's people, their children, their children's children, and so on down through the ages would have known

Him the same way. Innocence and holiness would have escalated instead of decreasing.

See and know the importance of following His plan for our lives; submitting, and trusting, as His beauty is encompassing our days that will bring His fullness, and His lifeblood to us and through us.

1 Now when Solomon had finished praying, fire came down from heaven and consumed the burnt offering and the sacrifices; and the glory of the Lord filled the temple.

2 And the priests could not enter the house of the Lord, because the glory of the Lord had filled the Lord's house.

10 On the twenty-third day of the seventh month he sent the people away to their tents, joyful and glad of heart for the goodness that the Lord had done for David, for Solomon, and for His people Israel.

II Chronicles 7:1, 2, 10

Light came and overran darkness. Sin had no place to fester and grow. His people lived longer and, better with prosperity as a common factor throughout His nation. Life became full. Joy abounded! See His glory, His temple, the beauty of His radiating presence! Oh Beloved, take hold from His point of view! Come up to where the I AM is and see this. Know I AM is in control. Hasten to do this.

His Most Holy Place was filled with His beautiful Light, the Father's Light, bouncing in every direction all at once, constantly, living, pure Light! God's glory resounds off the gold (we are His gold, His 'precious metal'), and He even made the place on fire with Himself.

And, yes, there is a preparation time before coming in. The priests prepared themselves, sanctified themselves. There is no need for discouragement and no need to push. I Am is with us daily, working a work to sanctify, prepare, and make beautiful. He will not turn us away and we are not to make a formula out of this time, but rather bask in His glory and His perfect beauty. Listen to His voice. Stay with Him on this and we will be changed, quickened into His likeness by His glory.

The room, the temple building was inundated with God's Shekinah glory as a thick cloud of moisture mixed with Oil, Life, and Light that flesh could not penetrate but rather was changed by being in His presence. Such unmistakable beauty lives within His holiness. His beauty inside and out!

Allow Father God to show you His temple, through His heart, His eyes. Watch and see, as you lay all emotions aside, and submit to Him, Beloved. Allow Him to show you how this holy building was, then He will reveal how His Living Temple, made with Living Stones, will be.

God put His plan in David's heart and David gave it to his son, as the Father directed. Solomon never knew defeat, he only knew greatness. He was David's heir and so much like him, however, King Solomon's time was a time of peace. He was as courageous as his father was, yet never went to battle. It was as though God took that courage and rerouted it to building His kingdom and enhancing His greatness with His beauty here on this earth.

Note: Solomon was unique in that he was so devoted to serving his Lord, he was used to being in His presence. When he yielded to idols, he automatically thought God would not react. He was sure the Lord wouldn't mind, though God's law of retribution was automatic. His mercy was always there, but Solomon didn't think he needed it because he knew the Father's love so well.

Solomon built God a temple, a holding place, for Him here, on earth. How He longs to fill us with His glory, just as He did Solomon's temple, to express just how beautiful He is. Let us be a holding place for Your beauty, O Lord as we submit to Your Shekinah presence. His temple was filled with a radiating love that poured from the gold. The walls were alive with His love. Gold, pure gold is translucent and seemingly unending. The thickness of the overlaid gold on the perfect cedar and cypress seemed to be liquid, with much depth. God gave David these plans to leave a blueprint for this time and these days, to establish His true Living Temple; His Most Holy Place made of Living Stones. When God's Shekinah presence filled Solomon's temple pure light was everywhere, bouncing back and forth upon itself! Pure Light, Living Light, THE Light of the World, THE Life Source, The Son, expressed Himself in that Most Holy Place. We will see this, again, as God reveals new colors, as His pure Light source radiates throughout His glory to us, His Living Temple. His Light restores us to wholeness. A new thing does He do. NOW it shall spring forth. No fear, only vision, greatness, beauty, a new road, a new river. See His BEAUTY!

Attribute #2
Temple <u>Covenant</u> to be Restored

12 Then the Lord appeared to Solomon by night, and said to him: "I have heard your prayer, and have chosen this place for Myself as a house of sacrifice.

13 "When I shut up heaven and there is no rain, or command the locusts to devour the land, or send pestilence among My people,

14 "if My people who are called by My name will humble themselves, and pray and seek My face and turn from their wicked ways, then I will hear from heaven, and will forgive their sin and heal their land.

15 *"Now My eyes will be open and My ears attentive to prayer made in this place.*

16 *"For now I have chosen and sanctified this house, that My name may be there forever; and My eyes and My heart will be there perpetually.*

17 *"As for you, if you walk before me as your father David walked, and do according to all that I have commanded you, and if you keep My statutes and My judgments,*

18 *"then I will establish the throne of your kingdom, as I covenanted with David your father, saying, 'You shall never fail to have a man as ruler in Israel.'*

19 *"But if you turn away and forsake My statutes and My commandments which I have set before you, and go and serve other gods, and worship them,*

20 *"then I will uproot them from My land which I have given them; and this house which I have sanctified for My name I will cast out of My sight, and will make it to be a proverb and a byword among all nations.*

21 *"And as for this house, which is exalted, everyone who passes by it will be astonished and say, 'Why has the Lord done thus to this land and this house?'* — Generations

22 *"Then they will answer, 'Because they forsook the Lord God of their fathers, who brought them out of the land of Egypt, and embraced other gods, and worshipped them and served them; therefore He has brought all this calamity on them.'"* **II Chronicles 7: 12-22**

33

God's covenant was set in place for His chosen, His hand picked nation, to reign victoriously on this earth. He chose Jerusalem for His dwelling place and this people to rule, and He chose this man, Solomon, to take the place of God's beloved David. The Lord's word went forth with rules and guidelines for covenant living in His kingdom here on earth. All was well.

Note: The only part of God that does not hold a condition is His love, which is unconditional. His love is always the same, always, no matter what, and His love will never fail nor come to an end, because He IS Love.

Father God proclaimed a covenant to Solomon that night to abide by throughout his reign and to be carried down through the ages, to us, so all would be holy and prosper and be in health, so His glory would have a place to dwell in regularly. God's goal was to establish a place, a people, and a time to begin the rest of their days (and ours) on earth in victory and in godliness, to bring all into His fullness, and completeness of who I AM is. All was in place. EVERYTHING was set in order as the temple was completed. He even made provision for sin to be forgiven. God never wanted a king to rule. He wanted to rule by His own hand; however, the people wanted a king, so He granted their request. Ultimately, what they chose destroyed them, their families, communities, and their peace and drove their God away.

The covenant was set in place with the dedication of the temple. Every provision had been established, in order, if only His king and His people who were called by His name had humbled themselves and turned from idolatry, pride, and their manmade gods. They fell so easily because everything was so good. Solomon forgot Who made him prosperous. He forgot where his wisdom came from. Father God let him go a long way before He pulled his kingdom down. Solomon knew he was in sin, however, at that point in time, he loved his gods more than he loved his God. He died knowing the legacy he left behind.

In this Temple made of Living Stones, this Temple that is alive and growing and expanding, God's name and His King, The King of kings, is here forever. His eyes and His heart are here perpetually. Moreover, yes, this Temple is being sanctified continually, and is made holy, continually.

If My people, who have been called by My name humble themselves, pray, seek My face and turn from their wicked ways, then will I hear and heal and restore and make you worthy of carrying My Name, My Shekinah presence. My fire will be in you and will burn wherever you go. My people, created in My likeness, humble yourselves, pray without ceasing, turn to Me, My face, My living Word, and live My word, turn from your wicked ways to My holy ways. Be holy even as I am holy.

Attribute #3
Temple <u>Wealth</u> to be Restored

23 So King Solomon surpassed all the kings of the earth in riches and wisdom.

24 And all the earth sought the presence of Solomon to hear his wisdom, which God had put in his heart.

25 Each man brought his present: articles of silver and gold, garments, armor, spices, horses, and mules, at a set rate year by year. **I Kings 10:23-25**

1 Now when the queen of Sheba heard of the fame of Solomon concerning the name of the Lord, she came to test him with hard questions.

2 She came to Jerusalem with a very great retinue, with camels that bore spices, very much gold, and precious stones; and when she came to Solomon, she spoke with him about all that was in her heart.

3 So Solomon answered all her questions; there was nothing so difficult for the king that he could not explain it to her.

4 And when the queen of Sheba had seen all the wisdom of Solomon, the house that he built,

5 the food on his table, the seating of his servants, the service of his waiters and their apparel, his cupbearers, and his entryway by which he went up to the house of the Lord, there was no more spirit in her. **I Kings 10:1-5**

7b "Your wisdom and prosperity exceed the fame of which I heard.

8 "Happy are your men and happy are these your servants, who stand continually before you and hear your wisdom!

9 "Blessed be the Lord your God, who delighted in you, setting you on the throne of Israel! Because the Lord has loved Israel forever, therefore He made you king, to do justice and righteousness."

10 Then she gave the king one hundred and twenty talents of gold, spices in great abundance, and precious stones. There never again came such abundance of spices as the queen of Sheba gave to King Solomon.

I Kings 10:7b-10 (Queen of Sheba speaking)

15a Also the king made silver and gold as common in Jerusalem as stones... **II Chronicles 1:15a**

20 Judah and Jerusalem were as numerous as the sand by the sea in multitude, eating and drinking and rejoicing.

24 For he had dominion over all the region on this side of the River from Tiphsah even to Gaza, namely over all the kings on this side of the River; and he had peace on every side all around him.

26 Solomon had forty thousand stalls of horses for his chariots, and twelve thousand horsemen.

27b There was no lack in their supply.
I Kings 4:20, 24, 26, 27b

15 This is the reason for the labor force which King Solomon raised: to build the house of the Lord, his own house, the Millo, the wall of Jerusalem, Hazor, Megiddo, Gezer. **Kings 9:15**

The temple was a holding place for His very presence, God's glory. This Most Holy Place held the Great I AM, THE Majestic God of ALL the earth for all, who were sanctified and made righteous, to drink from. The children of Israel would come to the temple and be filled with His presence and then go out to their places to make their homes and families and communities prosperous, always, not just sometimes. This was a way of living. There were no hardships as long as Solomon did what was right in God's sight. The Father's eyes were on the Most Holy Place day and night, to oversee, to protect, and to bless. The wealth that was there was as common as the beauty that was there and the joy and the unity and the love. This is His character; His name is Jehovah Jireh. His glory ran from the temple, as a river, into the streets, the villages, the land, shops, governments, work-places, and wealth ran with it. See God's Kingdom come on earth, His Living Temple, as prosperity is restored to His Body.

Solomon was not a special person. He was born into the family line to become king. He answered the call and built God a house. It was not the structure that caught the Father's eye, it was Solomon's motivation. God longed for a place to inhabit so His people could gather, as one, to worship the Most High. Solomon wanted to give God the best, because that was how he knew Him, as the Best God of all gods. God, in turn, gave what He had. He only has the best. He does not have less or little or some, He has the best, the most, and the greatest. See the Temple made of stone, and then envision the greatness of His plan restored to the Living Temple. Blessings of wealth spilled out, and overflowed from His sanctuary to wherever His people went and onto whatever their task was. God made gold and silver as abundant as stones. The entire heathen, uncircumcised nations saw the God Solomon and the people of Israel served and were jealous.

The Spirit of prosperity, God Himself, attracts the wealthy. God's wisdom was seen and brought in wealth. Noblemen, kings, the Queen of Sheba could not help but give, to impress Solomon. They could not resist God's anointing of wealth that was upon the king. They were so moved that they gave what they had. It brought wealth into God's temple. Storage places were set up all around Jerusalem, as treasuries. God's people were never without and always gave, as did their king.

God's glory and wealth go hand in hand.

Attribute #4
Joy to be Restored

10 On the twenty-third day of the seventh month he sent the people away to their tents, joyful and glad of heart for the goodness that the Lord had done for David, for Solomon, and for His people Israel. **II Chronicles 7:10**

65 At that time Solomon held a feast, and all Israel with him, a great congregation from the entrance of Hamath to the Brook of Egypt, before the Lord our God, seven days and seven more days—fourteen days.

66 On the eighth day he sent the people away; and they blessed the king, and went to their tents joyful and glad of heart for all the goodness that the Lord had done for His servant David, and for Israel His people. **I Kings 8:65, 66**

God's whole nation joined in; all were joyful and merry in heart. What a sight to see! There was not a sad, downtrodden, sorrowful one in the hundreds of thousands. Every tribe was there, all His priests, His prophets;

the WHOLE nation was there. The builders, the scribes, all the leaders, of course the king, the children, oh the children, the elders became as children. There was no death in this assembly in God's Holy Temple, only life. Joy abounded, pure joy, just as the gold was pure, the joy was pure also. Such power in one place! In millions, absolute pure, holy power as His life was flowing through His nation, a holy consecrated people. ALL came to exalt Him, to pay tribute to their Lord. In this consecration, during these days of sacrificing, giving and giving, AND GIVING, love poured forth from earth to the heavens. God's temple, built with human hands, was FILLED WITH JOY. Grasp the exuberance in His temple. His pure love was there resounding as a force throughout the walls, the floors, the articles, the sacrifices, and the instruments.

The instruments dripped with His oil of gladness.

This celebration changed the environment. The people went to their neighborhoods, their homes, and their jobs, totally consumed in His joy and His love. They gathered before the Great Lord Jehovah to give Him what they had. He accepted this sacrifice of selflessness and gave back what He had, Himself; Joy and Love. God's joy and love go hand in hand. God is joy, a fruit of the Spirit, so when He is present, joy is present.

As we purpose to rid ourselves of listlessness and apathy we receive all the Lord has for us.

JOY unspeakable will abound!

Solomon built this house for God's presence to come into and live all the time. His priests would represent the people. They would offer prayers and sacrifices daily This kept the temple alive with HIM as joy was always in this in place; His glory too.

God's joy is not happiness. Happiness is of the soul. The joy of the Holy Spirit lives on forever and is present even when pressure comes from the evil one. Happiness, however, flees quickly.

 God's nation praised and worshipped Him with one voice, in perfect unity, which strengthened the atmosphere to bring Himself to them. The people made a place for joy to reverberate and explode. The senses were touched, though joy did not start in the senses. They soon were filled to the full with jubilation.

What a time of sanctification and holiness before the Lord!

When we become sanctified, the senses also become sanctified, resulting in the most gratifying experience the body could ever have, within His protection of holiness. Our spirit rules the senses, relates and dictates to the flesh. The perfectness of the Creator presses into the five physical senses, thus affecting the body, the mind, and the emotions. Sound, color, scent, touch, and taste are all heightened and alive, responding to the Most High. The trumpeters, the singers, all who worshipped and sang out

His praises, heard with sanctified ears, heavenly music, pure voices, and holy sounds coming from the people and their instruments.

The fragrance of the temple enhanced the joy. As years went by, that fragrance stayed with them in their memories. During times of upheaval and bondage, God's people would remember the fragrance that came from the temple and weep. They would be so homesick.

As His joy filled His nation, His temple, colors came alive in that place. The purples, blues and crimson; the gold and brass on the instruments all took His life to them and paraded themselves throughout the place. The colors of each tribe became a part of this grand gathering. The elders eyes danced for glee and sparks of glory connected one to the other. This was not a tradition taken lightly. His people planned for that time. They thought of nothing else. JOY UNSPEAKABLE AND FULL OF GLORY!

God filled His people with His food. They tasted Him and proclaimed it was good! O, what joy, what love!

As they rejoiced and embraced one another; tribe to tribe, priest to priest, elder to elder, father to children, mother to son, all became one, all were in perfect unity. His presence, His hand would rest upon them, and yes, they would fall to the ground rejoicing, come up praising, worshiping their Lord Jehovah. Then they would touch another in holiness and in a STRIKE OF

GLORY, loose themselves to His touch, and find themselves, once more, overcome in His glory. God's joy consumed the temple!

Attribute #5
Unity to be Restored

6 Also King Solomon, and all the congregation of Israel who were assembled with him before the ark, were sacrificing sheep and oxen that could not be counted or numbered for multitude.

13 indeed it came to pass, when the trumpeters and singers were as one, to make one sound to be heard in praising and thanking the Lord, and when they lifted up their voice with the trumpets and cymbals and instruments of music, and praised the Lord, saying:

"For He is good, for His mercy endures forever," that the house, the house of the Lord, was filled with a cloud,

14 so that the priests could not continue ministering because of the cloud; for the glory of the Lord filled the house of God. **II Chronicles 5:6, 13, 14**

A song of David, Solomon's father that was heard often in the congregation, proclaiming unity and bringing forth God's hand to bless His people:

1 Behold, how good and how pleasant it is,
for brethren to dwell together in unity!
2 It is like the precious oil upon the head,
running down on the beard,
the beard of Aaron,
running down on the edge of his garments.
3 It is like the dew of Hermon,
descending upon the mountains of
Zion;
For there the Lord commands the blessing —
Life evermore. **Psalm 133**

God's plan was to bring in His Shekinah presence so all would be in unity during this time of prosperity.

Unity has its rewards. It is evident to establish the fact that this was the one time, the beginning, for the Lord to set His Holy Nation, in order, in this earth, and unity was a vital part to bringing His greatness to the forefront for that time as well as the future. All was in place. The temple was built, the ark was brought in, the priests were sanctified, and sacrifices, without number, were in progress. His children, the whole nation of Israel, were all there. Expectation was at its peak! Such a force of unity, bringing in God's power, as worship was the glue that kept everyone focused on Him, the Great Lord Jehovah. He was so at one with His creation, that day! All things were possible! There was no lack, there was no sickness, and there was no death, only <u>life and life to the fullest</u>. Father God could do nothing else but display Himself to the ones who yearned to fellowship with their Lord as He consumed the sacrifices with a blast from His nostrils! It just took one blast of approval and fire came to His temple. All celebrated the Lord God Almighty. It made Him so happy, so satisfied. Had the children of Israel asked for anything, <u>anything</u>, He would have given it to them. All they could think of, though, was to please their Lord, to bring Him joy, and to give up whatever they had for Him. This was a good thing! That day God rejoiced over them with gladness and proclaimed blessing over His children through Solomon, blessings that have yet to be fulfilled. This proclamation is still alive, though doormat, waiting for His Beloved to gather, once again in <u>perfect unity</u>, and release God's blessings to this earth.

Unity strengthened the children of Israel for the days ahead. They never forgot the love of being one with the another. His tribes dropped their differences. The priests were all in one accord. That was their goal. They made a covenant to the Lord and to one another to stay consecrated before Him day and night. God's Chosen gave freely to one another after this day. They became selfless. They had all things in common. Husbands and wives had peace in their homes. Merchants were at one with the other and helped one another to prosper. <u>Love abounded</u>

through this life force, unity. The enemy had no place to come in and conquer because unity had strengthened the children of Israel.

When God released His fire that day, nations all around Jerusalem could see this great light. They were terrified at this display of power and became even more terrified when they heard Who sent it. Oh! He must have laughed at this!

The Lord longs to show Himself off in these last days with demonstrations of His power. We must watch and pray and work at unifying God's Holy Nation.

Attribute #6
Worship to be Restored

6 Also King Solomon, and all the congregation of Israel who were assembled with him before the ark, were sacrificing sheep and oxen that could not be counted or numbered for multitude,

11 And it came to pass when the priests came out of the Most Holy Place (for all the priests who were present had sanctified themselves, without keeping to their divisions),

12 and the Levites who were the singers, all those of Asaph and Heman and Jeduthun, with their sons and their brethren, stood at the east end of the altar, clothed in white linen, having cymbals, stringed instruments and harps, and with them one hundred and twenty priests sounding with trumpets——

13 indeed it came to pass, when the trumpeters and singers were as one, to make one sound to be heard in praising and thanking the Lord, and when they lifted up their voice with the trumpets and cymbals and instruments of music, and praised the Lord saying: "For He is good, For His mercy endures forever," that the house, the house of the Lord, was filled with a cloud,

14 so that the priests could not continue ministering, because of the cloud; for the glory of the Lord filled the house of God. **II Chronicles 5:6, 11-14**

13b and he (Solomon) *stood on it, knelt down on his knees before all the congregation of Israel, and spread out his hands toward heaven,*

14 and said: "Lord God of Israel, there is no God in heaven or on earth like You, who keep Your covenant and mercy with Your servants who walk before You with all their hearts." **II Chronicles 6:13b-14**

1 Now when Solomon finished praying, fire came down from heaven and consumed the burnt offering and the sacrifices; and the glory of the Lord filled the temple.

2 And the priests could not enter the house of the Lord, because the glory of the Lord filled the Lord's house.

3 When all the children of Israel saw how the fire came down, and the glory of the Lord on the temple, they bowed their faces to the ground on the pavement, and worshiped and praised the Lord, saying:

"For He is good, For His mercy endures forever."
II Chronicles 7:1-3

Worship was <u>set</u> in the temple, at this time, when the multitude of voices went up to the Lord. Their hearts came before Him that day. The sound of the trumpets, the sound of the voices, and the sound of the stringed instruments all came before Him as a living piece of woven lacework that glowed and sang and radiated God's Shekinah presence. The Lord saw their worship stretch across the heavenlies. It was enormous, grand in display, and sparks of glory were constantly being released into the galaxies. Worship sounded and resounded, resonated continually and lasted for days. His heavenly creatures responded, in worship, in absolute joy and, of course, love blew into the skies making all creation <u>one.</u> The trees were one with the oceans. The earth was one with the air. All life responded to life and all was in order.

There is unity in worship! This very powerful force, worship, produces life, love, peace, strength, and HIM!

See why we must worship in the Spirit of holiness. Then will His perfect presence come to us and ours in these last days. In these last days, Father God will display, across the heavenlies, signs, and wonders that will be ignited by worship. He is ordering, even now, orchestrated times of worship across this earth. As the Spirit calls us to stop what we are doing and worship the Lord, know He is calling others, from the East, the West, the North and the South to worship at the same time! The same words are released with the same instruments, the same sound, the same beat, the same heartbeat, exploding His glory into this earth. This will be a sign and a wonder to the nations and a welcome relief to the Beloved.

This is a declaration of freedom for all to glory in.

His kingdom come on earth as it is in heaven. All heaven joins together constantly, in praise and worship, whenever the call is ignited. God's holy nation must worship Him CONTINUALLY, here on earth. Why? So His Glory, Himself, will be released wherever we are. And, He wants us to practice for heaven. Also, just because He wants us to. HE LOVES THIS! Worship is proclaiming who I AM is and acknowledging God's greatness, forgetting ourselves, and wanting to be with our Lord, just because of Who He is.

Yes, this is intimacy with our First Love. It is creative! When worship goes to God, He takes it and creates substance with it. Worship comes before Him as a receptacle, a container. He then fills it with Himself responding to our needs, wants, and desires. He fills our worship containers with miracles as we worship Him in Spirit and in truth.

Attribute #7
Glory to be Restored

13 ...to make one sound to be heard in praising and thanking the Lord... ...that the house, the house of the Lord, was filled with a cloud,

14 so that the priests could not continue ministering, because of the cloud; for the glory of the Lord filled the house of God. **II Chronicles 5:13-14**

1 Now when Solomon finished praying, fire came down from heaven and consumed the burnt offering and the sacrifices; and the glory of the Lord filled the temple.

2 And the priests could not enter the house of the Lord, because the glory of the Lord had filled the Lord's house.

3 When all the children of Israel saw how the fire came down, and the glory of the Lord on the temple, they bowed their faces to the ground on the pavement, and worshiped and praised the Lord... **II Chronicles 7:1-3**

God has chosen us His Living Temple, at this hour, to pour His glory into. As Bloodwashed believers, we have His glory in us. **John 17:22a,** Jesus speaking, *"And the glory which You gave Me I have given them..."*.

However, these are the days, this is the time for God to show us His Shekinah glory, in a grand display, as was seen in Solomon's Temple. We must receive His mercy and patience, with much reverential fear, as we prepare to receive the fullness of His glory. He sees our hearts and hears our cries that long for more of Him. Know that as sons and daughters of the Most High God, He works with us, as we listen with our spirits, and allow the Lord to sanctify. We must know Him in intimacy, all the time, so we can move easily in His Shekinah presence to be healed and made whole and then to work His miracles.

These are the days of new beginnings. Foundational truths are being laid down and reinforced so God's glory will not be exploited or manipulated. When, of old, He displayed His glory, it was due to the condition of the time as the people prepared themselves for Him. The Lord carried the children of Israel through the sanctification process just as He carries us through; a preparation, a work in righteousness, a time of discipline and obedience and denial, a laying down of self to take up His fullness. Wherever God's Shekinah presence was poured out, there was much work beforehand as Israel sacrificed the offering of giving their best. (This too must be a time of selflessness.) Worship lasted past the ordinary time, as prayers and worship reached the Most High. It seemed unending. The flesh had no room to complain or rule. His order is to bring us back to those times, quickly, so His glory will envelope His people as a new thing, a refreshing, a reviving, a restoring, a rest, with much joy, and display of His power.

Only God's glory can usher in this last move of His Spirit upon this earth. Woe to those who make a tradition of this time. Woe to those who would make a denomination out of this time. Woe to those who try to sell this move. Woe to those who take this time, this move for granted as judgment will be their reward. In His presence is fullness of joy. In God's glory, there is fullness of joy. Oh, how He longs to bathe us as we bask in His pool of glory in our homes as well as in the sanctuary. He longs to become more intimate with us and show Himself to us to bring us closer to Him and up higher into His Throne Room.

We must allow Father God to minister to us in these next days so we will know how to receive His Shekinah presence, walk in it, and work His work. This is where ALL needs are met. Take rest in His glory. Allow His hand to rest upon you moving you onwards and upwards into His Shekinah Glory!

Attribute #8
Temple Government to be Restored

7 (Solomon speaking) *"Now, O Lord my God, You have made Your servant king instead of my father David,*

but I am a little child; I do not know how to go out or come in.

9 "Therefore give to Your servant an understanding heart to judge Your people, that I may discern between good and evil. For who is able to judge this great people of Yours?"

10 And the speech pleased the Lord, that Solomon had asked this thing.

11 Then God said to him: "Because you have asked this thing, and have not asked long life for yourself, nor have asked riches for yourself, nor have asked the life of your enemies, but have asked for yourself understanding to discern justice,

12a "behold, I have done according to your words; see, I have given you a wise and understanding heart ..."
I Kings 3: 7, 9-12a

1 So King Solomon was king over all Israel.

7 And Solomon had twelve governors over all Israel, who provided food for the king and his household; each one made provision for one month of the year.

20 Judah and Israel were as numerous as the sand by the sea in multitude, eating and drinking and rejoicing. (5-6 million)

21 So Solomon reigned over all kingdoms from the River to the land of the Philistines, as far as the border of Egypt. They brought tribute and served Solomon all the days of his life.

22 Now Solomon's provision for one day was thirty kors of fine flour, sixty kors of meal (195,72 bu.),

23 ten fatted oxen, twenty oxen from the pastures, and one hundred sheep, besides deer, gazelles, roebucks and fatted fowl.

24b. . . .and he had peace on every side all around him.

25 And Judah and Israel dwelt safely, each man under his vine and his fig tree, from Dan as far as Beersheba, all the days of Solomon. **Kings 4: 1, 7, 20, 21-25**

3 "You know how my father David could not build a house for the name of the Lord his God because of the wars which were fought against him on every side, until the Lord put his foes under the soles of his feet.

4 "But now the Lord my God has given me rest/peace on every side, so that there is neither adversary nor evil occurrence." **I Kings 5:3-4**

Solomon knew his limitations in ruling over such a people as Israel. He was young in experience. He watched his father rule and was confident in the God of his father because Solomon saw David walk out his relationship with his God, knowing he was nothing without Him. Solomon knew his work would be futile if Yahweh was not first in his life. It changed the course of nations. He prospered in everything he touched because he would spend his days seeking God's way of doing and being right. He ran a righteous government. God, indeed, granted the king wisdom to oversee the government. Solomon, however, maintained the link that kept him tied into hearing and receiving. He knew his power source and was in constant communication with His Lord about daily affairs in government. The Lord would tell him of things to come to ward off catastrophes that could harm his people. In short, it was profitable for Solomon to bring God into the 'oval office' every day. Israel prospered and was at peace because their king was a righteous man. Righteous living spilled over to those that encompassed his daily routine. The more responsibility Solomon had, the greater the opportunity afforded him to change his world. The same goes to us, His Righteous, today.

King Solomon surrounded himself with twenty-three trustworthy men, to help oversee the government and administer peace and well-being in his kingdom. He knew the task at hand was greater than what he could ever accomplish by himself. He saw the wisdom of God come forth as he added the men he needed to his cabinet. He chose men far beyond his understanding, recognizing the fruit of his asking for wisdom that night the Lord appeared to him in a dream.

Eleven officials were placed in eleven strategic positions: one as high priest; two secretaries; one official historian in charge of record keeping; a commander-in-chief to oversee his army; two priests; one secretary of state over the officers; one manager of palace affairs; one supervisor of public works; and Solomon's good friend as priest and personal advisor. Twelve governors were chosen, one from every tribe, to serve the king in providing provision for him and his court. Each was given the privilege of arranging provision for one month out of the year. The choices were made with accuracy and the matches were accomplished with much precision. Whether they were men of valued reputation, trustworthy friends, or family, all worked in total harmony at serving their king, their country, and their God. Solomon saw the wisdom of God pour out of him and into his governors and cabinet members, as extensions of his authority. He knew he had asked for a good thing the night he asked for wisdom to rule his people, and because of this God-given choice, there was peace and safety, unity within the ranks, and neither internal rebellion nor external upheaval was to be found.

Throughout all the lifetime of Solomon, all of Judah and Israel lived in peace and safety; and each family had its own home and garden. **I Kings 4:25** TLB

What a contrast between David's reign and Solomon's. David had enemies and wars on every side of him, however, God gave Solomon rest and peace on every side of him, yet both had one goal, to build a House, a Holy Temple, as a dwelling place for their Lord Jehovah. David won the battles and Solomon established a safe and righteous government for the people of Israel.

Solomon could not have accomplished all the great things that he did had it not been for a strong, well-built government. There were so many times when he could have failed at bringing forth the perfect plan had it not been for God's wisdom and the group of godly men encompassed about him. He had much respect from all the kings of the surrounding nations because they not only saw his wisdom, but also saw how his nation was run, in such perfect unity and harmony.

And men of all nations, from all the kings of the earth who had heard of his wisdom, came to hear the wisdom of Solomon. **I Kings 4:34**

There was great joy in every day events. This was a direct outcome of the internal God Who controlled every event, whether it be a sale at the local market, building roads or greeting the Queen of Sheba as she came in all her regalia, to hold court with the notable and mighty King Solomon. She saw the way he handled his servants.

Their joy and peace was prosperity to her. She heard of his accomplishments and how great a population he ruled over.

There was peace, joy and an abundant lifestyle for all who lived under Solomon's reign all the days he was on this earth. He cried out to his heavenly Father, in his inadequacy, asking for wisdom to govern the millions under his care. The Lord not only gave him wisdom, but also riches and honor.

"And I have also given you what you have not asked: both riches and honor, so that there shall not be anyone like you among the kings all your days." **I Kings 3:13**

He proved God's power as he allowed Him to display Himself; in government making decisions, in wealth, in integrity, in beauty, in creativity and in ordinary daily activities. As Solomon walked in God's provision he was also preparing his people to do the same. He was their example of how to rule and reign, in total authority, as a servant of the Most High God. His people emanated their leader.

Solomon was king for four years before he started to build the temple. During that time, he corrected mistakes and strengthened weaknesses within his appointed cabinet. He saw a great nation become sanctified and thirst after righteousness and holiness. Unity and peace grew and became the main catalyst to the gathering of the workers who would eventually spend seven years building the Most Holy Place, the House of the Lord. They would do this, not out of duty, but rather out of love and service for their Lord and their king Solomon. What a perfect place and what a perfect time to build a holy habitation for the Living God, Lord Jehovah. The building of the temple would only strengthen the government because whenever the people would go in to worship, His Shekinah presence would pour out and fill the people. They, in turn, would bring His glory to their work places and their homes. God gave Solomon everything that was needed, in abundance, not only to build this structure, but also He gave provision for their daily needs. Wealth abounded as the building began. The children of Israel were successful socially, economically, and spiritually.

Expect a Change

As Solomon prepared his people to build the temple, so too is the Holy Spirit preparing His people to rebuild the Living Temple. The walls have been broken down and lay in ruin. Many plans and dreams have gone unfinished and seemingly forsaken. However, in these last days, expect! Look for our Lord God to make expedient reversals. Where there was no provision for change, there will be an immediate provision for change. For, these are the hours when the first will be become the last, and the last, first, so that the children of the Most High can take their rightful positions, entering into the rest and peace that for too long, have been held up. Expect; look for the season of enormous wealth and well being exploding upon the Living Temple, the Body of Christ, as a great tidal wave of the Glory of our God hits this earth. Only because of the resurrection power that lives within each beloved saint, the lifeblood of Jesus Christ, do we have the provision to answer the call in these last, of the last days. The Blood of Jesus is calling, crying out, and beckoning the Body to wake up, shake off the numbness and apathy, and repent to a higher calling of grace, power, and provision. He is calling for a preparation that can only be accomplished through a change of heart. The hour has come for the Living Temple, made without walls, to be at peace with their Lord and with one another. Be reconciled to each other. For too long this process has gone untouched and annulled. There is power in reconciliation. There is power in repentance. Solomon built the temple in total unity and correct placement. We must do the same. Backsliders, come home!

The wisdom of God put twenty-three men in key positions so Solomon could run his government, his nation, in righteousness and power. These are the days, NOW, when God is moving those out of high positions in government and economics, as He is beckoning His Holy Nation, the Body Of Christ, to come and take its rightful position, within the political and social spheres, to bring righteousness back to our land. No more are we to wait and see and say, "Maybe tomorrow..." but rather we must take the time, now, to prepare ourselves for the transformation and the transference of power and authority. Governmental positions, all of a sudden, will become available. All of a sudden you will be asked to take up those positions.

Get ready!

Expect!

Let it be known, not by your power nor your might but rather by the Spirit of the living, loving God a grand restoration in is process. Thy will be done, Thy Kingdom come on earth as it is in heaven!!!

Oh Beloved, make preparation to live in safety and peace and abundant provision, in Him!

Attribute #9
God's <u>Wisdom</u> to be Restored

7 "Now, O Lord my God, You have made Your ser-vant king instead of my father David, but I am a little child; I do not know how to go out or come in.

8 "And Your servant is in the midst of Your people whom You have chosen, a great people, too numerous to be numbered or counted.

9 "Therefore give to Your servant an understanding heart to judge Your people, that I may discern between good and evil. For who is able to judge this great people of Yours?"

10 And the speech pleased the Lord, that Solomon had asked this thing. **I Kings 3:7-10** (Solomon speaking)

7. Now, O Lord my God, You have made Your servant king instead of David my father, and I am but a lad (in wisdom and experience); I know not how to go out (begin) or come in (finish). **I Kings 3:7** AMP

Solomon knew who he was. He took his place willingly as servant of the Most High God. He also took his responsibilities as king. He knew he could not rule and reign in his own strength, his own powers. He only knew he was to be king over many, for his whole life. Solomon's ethics were that of his father, David. He was shown the task set before him and God put joy and excellence upon him. He was established, that day, as the greatest king, ever.

When Solomon asked for help, *therefore give Your servant an understanding heart to judge Your people...* **I Kings 3:9** he made a statement declaring that he could not do what was expected of him without God. The king was not a coward; he had much confidence in himself. He admitted, however, this work had past what he was capable of doing. He was a strong man and was very good at what he knew to do. What made him stronger was admitting he could not be king without God doing more, in him, than what He had done in the past.

The Son of God is wisdom. He is the living Word that dwells within the believer. When we ask for wisdom, we go to the reservoir and draw what we need that enables us to do the task at hand. This is resident within us always. However, the wisdom that is being restored to His Living Temple is being imparted to those who have been commissioned to special places for a specific work. God gave Solomon wisdom that was full of knowledge on how to rule a people, how to be clever in governmental affairs, applying justice so that all would prosper. This godly wisdom enabled the king to build a nation that exceeded the borders and boundaries of the past, and went through roadblocks and hindrances, bringing excellence to success and prosperity. Solomon needed the wisdom suited for a king. Not only did God give him wisdom; He gave him a generous spirit, a compassionate heart to see the need of the common person and how to fulfill it. The Lord gave him His heart to serve the people, all the days of his life. King Solomon was always thinking of ways to improve living conditions. He was constantly planning

for the future, with excitement and expectancy of greatness. He never thought of loss or failure. He knew that
with God, all things were possible, there were no limits.
Had he been on this earth today, Solomon would have
owned the moon and there would be no wars during his
rule. There would be no homeless. Everyone would be
successful. The heavenly Father gave Solomon the kind
of wisdom he needed to rule as king and He gave him
knowledge to discern good from evil, so good would
prevail and evil would have no place. He had largeness
of heart. The Queen of Sheba could not understand this
because it was not tangible. However, she saw the fruit
of it in watching the care and love his people had toward
their king. The people of Israel were devoted to Solomon
and served him with much joy and pleasure.

What do trees and animals and songs have to do with
wisdom to rule a great nation? *He spoke three thousand
proverbs, and his songs were one thousand and five. Also
he spoke of trees, from the cedar tree of Lebanon even
to the hyssop that springs out of the wall; he spoke also
of animals, of birds, of creeping things, and of fish.* **I
Kings 4: 32, 33** God placed in Solomon the wisdom to
attract all kinds of people. People from other cultures
were drawn to him because he knew so much and sometimes more about them and their environment than they
did themselves;

i.e. ...*the cedar trees of Lebanon.* Solomon would study everything he could about his guests, before they would arrive. He would have teachers come in, from foreign lands, to tell him about their countries. He was constantly asking his Lord to explain. He inquired of the Lord always.

For the Lord gives wisdom; From His mouth come knowledge and understanding; **Proverbs 2:6**

God was seen in him. Foreigners were drawn to him because they saw the wisdom of God within him. This brought great pleasure to the Father.

The great I AM is restoring specific wisdom back to His Living Temple, the Body of Christ. Each believer has a kind of wisdom stored up just for his/her task at hand. Solomon was great because he asked for help. We have the same potential for greatness as we step into our places that the Lord has prearranged for us. Step over into His provision of restoration now, and watch what will be done through a humble spirit, in the right place, at the right time, during these last days. God's restorative wisdom will be for the rest of our days. Solomon never ran out of this life source, but rather it became stronger and easier to work with, as he became more familiar in the working of Wisdom.

Chapter Three

This Living Temple Restored and You are a Part of it!

We have had a glimpse of King Solomon's Temple in all His glory, now, come see God's Living Temple the way He sees it. Oh, that we do not lean to our own understanding, but rather guide us Father, by Your Holy Spirit, into ALL truth.

13 But now in Christ Jesus, you who once were (so) far away, through (by, in) the blood of Christ have been brought near.

14 For He is (Himself) our peace (our bond of unity and harmony). He has made us both (Jew and Gentile) one (body)...

15b ...that He from the two might create in Himself one new man (one new quality of humanity out of the two), so making peace.

16 And (He designed) to reconcile to God both (Jew and Gentile, united) in a single body by means of His cross, thereby killing the mutual enmity and bringing the feud to an end.

19 Therefore you are no longer outsiders (exiles, migrants, and aliens, excluded from the rights of citizens), but you now share citizenship with the saints (God's own people, consecrated and set apart for Himself); and you belong to God's (own) household.

20 You are built upon the foundation of the apostles and prophets with Christ Jesus Himself the chief Cornerstone.

21 In Him the whole structure is joined (bound, welded) together harmoniously. and continues to rise, (grow, increase) into a holy temple in the Lord (a sanctuary dedicated, consecrated, and sacred to the presence of the Lord).

In Him (and in fellowship with one another) you yourselves also are being built up (into this structure) with the rest, to form a fixed abode (dwelling place) of God in (by, through) the Spirit. **Ephesians 2: 13-16, 19-22** AMP

15 By His death He ended the angry resentment between us... Then he took the two groups that had been opposed to each other and made them parts of Himself;

thus He fused us together to become one new person, and at last there was peace.

16 As parts of the same body, our anger against each other has disappeared, for both of us have been reconciled to God. And so the feud ended at last at the cross.

21 We who believe are carefully joined together with Christ as parts of a beautiful, constantly growing temple of God.

22 And you are also joined with Him and with each other by the Spirit, and are part of this dwelling place of God. **Ephesians 2:15, 16, 21, 22** TLB

5 (Come) and, like living stones, be yourselves built (into) a spiritual house, for a holy (dedicated, consecrated) priesthood, to offer up (those) spiritual sacrifices (that are) acceptable and pleasing to God through Jesus Christ. **I Peter 2:5** AMP

16 Do you not discern and understand that you (the whole church at Corinth) are God's temple (His sanctuary), and that God's Spirit has His permanent dwelling in you (to be at home in you, collectively as a church and also individually)? **I Corinthians 3:16**

This Living Temple is conjoined together in perfect harmony. It is a dwelling place for those who have been reconciled to their Creator, their Savior, and Chief

Cornerstone. His name is Jesus Christ. In Him we are hidden. In Him we are joined together to make a perfect Temple. Only in Him can a Temple of this proportion grow and expand and be beautiful and lovely and strong and well and pure. We are all welded together by Him, through Him, the Cornerstone, to this Living Temple. The Master Builder planned, before the foundation of time, this dwelling place for Himself. It is the Temple that breathes and emanates the lifeblood of Christ. Its strength comes from being bonded together in love and reinforced through unity. Love is the bond of perfection. Unity, harmony, and love work as mortar that joins each living stone to the other. This mortar, however, flows into each stone, keeping it alive, as does the circulatory system to the human body. As each living stone fellowships with the other, this Living Temple becomes stronger, more vibrant, and more recognizable.

Envision a group of young children, on a sunny, brisk, fall afternoon, racing as they play tag with one another. Each runs as quickly as possible to the other, laughing as they go, falling into the autumn leaves, getting up, and racing again to tag the next playmate. All the children become alert and alive, cheeks rosy, eyes brightened with excitement in the afternoon sun. They become bonded together by their playful time and somehow become closer, trusting one another in their simplicity. So too, does this time of camaraderie in fellowshipping within the Body of Christ, creating closeness and strengthening unity. It is a lifeline into eternity. Fellowship here, on earth, is the same as fellowship in heaven and is always centered on the Savior, the Chief Cornerstone, in full agreement and perfect unity. This is life and life to the fullest, in Him.

This Living Temple, this structure, is made of a divine calling. This holy place is not made of human hands, so no one can boast. This holy, Living Temple is made of grace. Its foundation is The Chief Cornerstone, The Rock of all ages. The bond of unity and harmony holds its stones together with love being the adhesive. Human eyes cannot see this. This Living Temple is made from the Blood of Christ Jesus. Look at the purity of the stones, no flaws in these gems. They are not to be tampered with. No flesh will take away what I AM has created here. We see the imperfections; God sees the outcome, the finished work, the perfectness. From the very beginning, He sees us whole, Father God sees the Body of Christ one with Him and one with each other.

20 "I do not pray for these alone, but also for those who will believe in Me through their word;

21 "that they all may be one, as You, Father, are in Me, and I in You; that they also may be one in Us, that the world may believe that You sent Me.

"I in them, and You in Me; that they may be made perfect in one..." **John 17: 20-21, 23a** (Jesus speaking)

Is He not one with us? Are we not one with the other, here, in His Kingdom? Why then do we spend time looking at the wrong, the disunity, and the brokenness? Rather, look to Him, worship Him and He will make us whole, one by one. When we fellowship with our Creator, we become strengthened and healed, thus strengthening the whole Living Temple. Only see the Light, not the darkness; only look for the finished work, not the brokenness. Yes, His Blood; we must plead the precious Blood of Jesus over His Body, the Living Temple so that His glory may be seen.

True Worship, Sanctification and Restoration

A call is being heard from deep within the Holy of Holies. A Voice that is so familiar, so gentle, yet authoritative with a cry for sanctification to live a life of true holiness and victory, to those who are called 'the Beloved' within the Body of Christ. Why now is there such urgency? It is as though God will not settle for anything less than 100% true worship from us. Why, now? What is so important or so critical? That gentle Voice is saying, "Me first. No more putting other things, people, or plans before Me. No idols, those manmade agendas

72

not of Me, that have been put first, placing Me second and taking your worship time away from Me. Even the lesser or smallest idol must go. All pride must go. Even a moment of pride ushers in the one who was thrown out of heaven. No more disobedience which leads to rebellion, pride, and idolatry." Is it that the demon forces are stronger than ever before, or is God calling for 100% of us? Perhaps we are not used to this kind of intense 'move of God'. The press is on with songs streaming from the sanctuary that cry out to God for more of His presence, asking for His glory to be seen and His power displayed in and through our lives.

We Are in 'Times of Restoration of All Things'

In these last days, the Father desires to 'restore all things' back to us, His Living Temple, and NOW is the time. He's coming soon for a church, triumphant, one without spot or wrinkle! We must be prepared and make room to receive all that He has for us in these end times. These are the days for the glorious Church to rise up! The Living, Holy Temple must be clean. It's restoration time!!!

19 "Repent therefore and be converted, that your sins may be blotted out, so that times of refreshing may come from the presence of the Lord,

20 "and that He may send Jesus Christ, who was preached to you before,

21 "whom heaven must receive until the times of restoration of all things, which God has spoken by the mouth of all His holy prophets since the world began."
Acts 3:19-21

Webster's definition of the word <u>restore</u> touches every area of our lives.
1. To restore, to give back something lost.
2. To restore, to bring back to a former or normal condition.
3. To restore, to put a person back in a place, position, or rank, etc.
4. To restore, to bring back health, strength.
5. To restore, to reestablish something which has passed away, as a custom, system of government, or society.

This word, <u>restore</u>, is so complete that it is all encompassing. God wants to touch our lives, healing our bodies, affecting our livelihoods, our positions, and our communities. Whether it be doctor, lawyer, teacher, plumber, builder, merchant, union worker, homemaker, garbage collector, millionaire, office worker, the student, the retired, the poor, the single parent, the homeless, the drug addict, the musician, or the minister, God wants to restore our lives, thus restoring His Holy Temple to its fullest.

It's Never Too Late With God

Maybe He wants you to become a basketball player. He wants us to become complete in what we're supposed to be. Some say, "It's too late. I'm fifty years old, too old to play basketball." Maybe so, however, He's not done with you. His desire is to repair, rebuild, and restore that which was taken away or ruined, by the thief, thus putting us into those positions, places, or ranks that we were supposed to have all along. A restoring of relationships, in family and society, is taking place as God heals our lives and makes us strong and whole in our bodies, in our minds and in our emotions.

A *Complete* Work is in Progress

What the thief has taken, when found out, he must restore back to us sevenfold. A rebuilding, a repairing to normal, in the supernatural, is in the works. Expect change! How long has the beloved, Body of Christ, been living in the 'second place' position, knowing this is not God's best? Our local governments, for too long, have been controlled by a cast of political thieves whose bloodline has contaminated the system for generations causing weakness, perversion in truth and plain ole' sin to rule and reign in our communities. As we stand righteous before the Lord, with the bond of unity one toward the other within the Living Temple, the one made without walls, we will make a difference in our communities, on our jobs, and in our government.

King Solomon wrote these words as he rejoiced over his city.

When it goes well with the righteous, the city rejoices; and when the wicked perish, there is shouting. By the blessing of the upright the city is exalted... **Proverbs 11:10, 11**

We all know the story. He was the richest, wisest king, EVER, EVER! Why? Because he was righteous, he was in right standing with his God and he took his rightful place. What and whom he believed in enveloped his life, his thinking, and his way of ruling the millions of people. We also are to make that kind of a difference in and through our lives. "Oh, but that was King Solomon!" you say. Oh, but we have been made the righteousness of God, in Christ Jesus. *For He made Him who knew no sin to be sin for us, that we might become the righteousness of God on Him.* **II Corinthians 5:21** We have THE King ruling and reigning in and through our lives. He already has made us victorious. Our task is to submit to our Most High God, be sanctified, so we can take our places across this land. We are living in the last of the last days and the Word, the prophetic, has been released, for all to take hold of with our faith, and expect our God to rule and reign as we watch His glory being released through His Holy Living Temple.

It's restoration time, Beloved!

Building the Temple of God Scriptures

20 But you, beloved, building yourselves up on your most holy faith, praying in the Holy Spirit, **Jude vs. 20**

6 As you have therefore received Christ Jesus the Lord, so walk in Him,

7 rooted and built up in Him and established in the faith, as you have been taught, abounding in it with thanksgiving. **Colossians 2:6-7**

21 in whom the whole building, being joined together, grows into a holy temple in the Lord,

22 in whom you also are being built together for a habitation of God in the Spirit. **Ephesians 2:21-22**

16 Do you not know that you are the temple of God and that the Spirit of God dwells in you? **I Corinthians 3:16**

Scripture Proclamation

I am constantly building myself up in my most holy faith, praying in the Spirit and I walk in Him, rooted and built up in Him and established in faith. I am joined together with the Body of Christ, in unity, as we all grow into a holy temple in the Lord.

Chapter Four

Loss: The Great Locust Invasion

✧

I n order to understand the degree and the extent of restoration, we must first see the degree of loss.

Grasp, get a picture of the devastation spoken of by
God's holy prophet, Joel, as he wrote of a destroying
army of locusts that was ...*strong and without number,
whose teeth are the teeth of a lion, and he has fangs of
a fierce lion.* **Joel 1:6.**

Torment was constant, unending for the children
of Zion who lived in the southern part of Judah during
the days of the great locust invasion. Hopelessness
could not describe the feeling as the people lost their
joy and reason for living to the destroying forces that
were everywhere. EVERYWHERE! The locusts came
in waves, as hungry, wild, crazed beasts who were
starving for food and drink. They would stop at nothing
until all was devoured, and ruined. The hard, laborious

work in harvesting the autumn crops became worthless because these crawling, biting, and consuming creatures devoured them. All the vines were stripped bare. The seed grain shriveled and dried up leaving no hope for future planting or harvests. The storehouses and barns were in shambles. Everywhere was heard the wailings of the people as they watched, in utter defenselessness, at the carnage. However, what was more mournful and sickening were the sounds of the beasts groaning in their emaciated fields. *The beasts of the field also cry to You, for the water brooks are dried up, and fire has devoured the open pastures.* **Joel 1:20** Even the land mourned at the ravage. The vines were dried up. All the trees were ruined, striped of their foliage, fruit, and bark, eaten, and then uprooted leaving nothing in its place except locust dung and dust. The times were unending and hateful without hope and without escape. The children had no food or water. The parents wept at this. The most innocent, simple pleasures had been invaded, tampered with, and overrun, leaving despair and loss. These locust creatures thought of nothing but destruction. Wave upon wave upon wave of locusts came and blackened the clear blue sky. As they flew, they released a fog of green mist-like powder that settled on anything and everything. Beauty could not be found. It had no more value.

Oh, how the Father must have wept as He longed to hear cries of repentance. Moreover, He did as the days ushered in a true repentance that lasted until the next wave of sin that brought in the enemy of the soul, rebellion. The locust's nature is stubborn and persistent and yes, devouring.

Joel 1:4 says, *"What the chewing locust has left, the swarming locust has eaten; what the swarming locust has left, the crawling locust has eaten; and what the crawling locust has left, the consuming locust has eaten."*

Each kind of locust represents a different kind of devastation, as each went about doing its specific task, the next would come behind doing theirs until the crops, the vegetation, the trees, the land, the water, the animals, the buildings and people were ravaged. The chewing locusts would bite, chew, and grind. The swarming locusts came in massive, teaming groups, covering every form of vegetation, smothering the life out of it. Then came the crawling locusts in slow motion. Like armored tanks, they took their time; meticulously devouring anything that was left, and then the consuming locusts landed with uncontrollable force, doing away with even the roots and stubble, until all was barren. Each kind of locust represents the thief as spoken of in John 10:10. Each has the plan to kill, steal, and destroy. They were invasive and mass-produced constantly. They would feed on anything they could chew.

It is a Promise from Our Lord

Times of revival are here with restoration set in place to the Beloved. Know that judgment is also set in place to the rebellious. In this last of the last days, restoration will only strengthen the Body of Christ, with no more loss, only gain. This time, these end times; ...*you shall eat in plenty and be satisfied. ...and My people shall not be put to shame* **Joel 2:26** IT'S A PROMISE FROM OUR LORD! A true revolution in godliness is in the making. All He wants is for us to be holy as He is holy and to be sanctified, ready to receive and ready to be used. We must keep our hearts with all diligence for out of it comes life and victory. Faith must prevail as victory enhances our lives all around us, thus changing our environment.

The loss was constant during those days of the locust invasion as spoken of by God's prophet, Joel. Look and see, imagine the loss. Then, look and see His promises to restore ALL to His Beloved. God's hand was upon Joel as he wrote what the Lord commanded him. The days of loss and destruction and chaos were in direct proportion to the sin that raced through the Father's 'holy' nation. Judgment was in place as an automatic response to sin, those undeniable acts done against God. However, the provision of reversing the curse was and always is in place as an absolute when repentance is brought into our lives and received in true humility. Repentance, a turning away from what is not acceptable to God, only enhances the greatness of His plan to subdue and bring low, so Himself has first place again. Joel wrote of a time when great devastation covered the land as a black cloud, with no way of restoring other than the hand of the Great Lord Jehovah moving in mercy and grace replenishing the earth with new hope and new life.

God promised that even the cattle would be restored, as new fields of grain sprang up suddenly. *Do not be afraid you beasts of the field; for the open pastures are springing up,* **Joel 2:22.** They ran through the pastures of green, as brand new calves, springing out of their stalls. Provision abounded!

Provision once again abounds as, in these last of the last days, His chosen come rejoicing, in true heartfelt repentance, and gratitude to their God as their Deliverer and Provider, once again, waters the earth with abundance. Father God is enhancing and is building up to a time that is called 'now', to withhold no good thing from those who walk uprightly before Him.

These are the days and the hours when restoration, a turning, replenishing, and revival, comes to all who are called His beloved Body of Christ. The Father restores to you the years. Oh no! Your time here has not ended and age has no factor during these last days. Conditions from the past that have to do with loss will be turned to plenty. The very thought of loss, the very sting of it will be as nothing. The years, the time, the human life span that has almost ended, will be restored. However, this is your choice. Choose this day life; extended, replenished, healed, and made whole.

Go on to greater and better, never the same as when, for so long, the devourer, the destroyer, the inhibitor controlled and subdued. God, Himself, restores. I AM is the One Who covenants peace with us, His Beloved. This covenant remains and strengthens as all is restored back. Look up! Get up! Wake up! Rise up to the next level so as to be in position for this time, now. For the years the locusts have destroyed are being replaced to you and yours. That's a promise! We must get in position, however, to receive. We must trust in GOD 100%. The times, they are changing. These are days of reversal, recompense and strengthening within the ranks. These are the years that are being restored.

God's regiment of time is equal to a thousand times a thousand and a million times a million days upon this earth all squeezed into these last days. His 'time' and our years are two different spans. His time is never lost, stolen, or perverted. God promises to restore ALL the years and ALL the loss in that time span that the locusts have stolen. Our loved ones will be blessed also because of His covenant of peace and restoration that we walk in. This will soften their hearts and bring true, lasting repentance. Watch and see as the Father restores. Your loved ones may have been watching you stumble, and they think you will stay like this, in a lower, downtrodden position and even worsen and then just die. However, I AM is restoring <u>ALL</u>.

God has promised full restoration of health, strength, joy, beauty, family, family values, position, credit, fame, houses, wealth and compassion, bringing miracles, godliness, education, wisdom, witty inventions, and more. ALL is being restored as repentance, grace and humility abounds to you and through you. They will see the God you serve and will have much respect for you.

Joel was compelled to announce repentance to all of Judah and Jerusalem. When they did, God restored the years that had been chewed up, wasted, and notably stolen. You have said, "Where have the years gone to? Where has the time gone?" The promise to restore the years has been written and is ours to claim and reclaim. As He reveals the loss to us, we will know what is to be replaced. Take stock. Make a list, without tears of sorrow, but rather with tears of joy, knowing what is in store for those who are called the Beloved. We must allow the Holy Spirit to guide us into all truth on these matters, so gently. Recount the loss, the theft, and even the things that are seemingly of little value and know ALL will be restored as His covenant of peace, the promise of restoration, rests upon us. They, the unbeliever, will see the peace we have. We will say, "It is good with my soul."

Come up to this expectancy, and release your faith as a lasso to victory. This has been prophesied for these days of great restoration ushering an awakening and THE last revival. Reclaim what is rightly yours as the Holy Spirit shows you more that is to be yours. Some will try to look back to where they were before and not be able to see who they were because so much has changed. Some will be so grafted to the Vine that the change will only draw them closer to the I AM. Some will forget who their God is and make their possessions their god. Woe to those who go after other gods to serve them.

Only look to your Creator, your Lord and your Restorer and REJOICE!

25 And I will restore or replace for you the years that the locust has eaten—the hopping locust, the stripping locust, and the crawling locust, My great army which I sent among you.

26 And you shall eat in plenty and be satisfied and praise the name of the Lord, your God, Who has dealt wondrously with you. And My people shall never be put to shame.

27 And you shall know, understand, and realize that I am in the midst of Israel and that I the Lord am your God and there is none else. My people shall never be put to shame. **Joel 2:25-27** AMP

The Word of the Lord

"Oh yes, I replace a time of mourning and heaviness and dryness and sighing with a time of joy, unspeakable, that is full of glory. Think of what has been taken away. Think of what has been stolen. Think of what never was but should have been. Think about the dreams that seemed so real but were not. Think about what stole your youth away from you. Think about, dare to recall the times when you said, "If only it were like this, I would have done it another way." These were the things that were stolen by the locusts. These were the times that were thwarted. So much has been shoved out of sight out of mind because the loss was too great to think of, so you just went on not expecting to get that which was lost back. These are the things, plans, and purposes that are to be restored to you and yours. Look around with your Spirit eyes and see what is due you. Hold on to My word, My plan, My time in time, and My purposes for this to happen.

A great reversal is in the working, to My, yes My Chosen. A great refreshing and wonderful time where My hand of grace is to be seen. Provision, wealth, restoration will be prevalent and because of this the soul will say it is good. Much joy will be heard in the camp. Days and nights of refreshing and fun and joy are in order. Oh, the joy of the Lord is your strength! This is for a three-fold purpose: 1. To fulfill prophecy. 2. My Body needs healing, strengthening, and rebuilding. I see this. I pro-vide My grace as a river, a wonderful flood coming over My Chosen. ③ The most hardened; critical unbeliever will see and will want to be included. This will bring My last revival to this earth."

Chapter Five

Preparation for Restoration Rend Your Heart

12 *"Now, therefore," says the Lord, "Turn to Me with all your heart, with fasting, with weeping, and with mourning."*

13a So, rend your heart, and not your garments; return to the Lord your God, **Joel 2:12-13a**

12 Therefore also now, says the Lord, turn and keep on coming to Me with all your heart, with fasting, with weeping, and with mourning (until every hindrance is removed and the broken fellowship is restored).

13a Rend your hearts and not your garments and return to the Lord, your God… **Joel 2: 12-13a** AMP

12 That is why the Lord says, "Turn to me now, while there is time. Give me all your hearts. Come with fasting, weeping, mourning.

13a Let your remorse tear at your hearts and not your garments." Return to the Lord your God...
Joel 2:12-13a TLB

'Once Upon A Time...'

Once upon a time, in the Kingdom of Light, God's Kingdom, the people of God, the brethren lived out their daily lives cooperating with an all too familiar demon called Complacency. This 'dragon' Complacency ruled over the people of God with an iron claw colored in shades of gray as fire-breathing words of self-righteousness, self-centeredness, and self-pity spewed from its mouth. Complacency would whine in the ears of the saints causing them to believe that God loves them so much that they could do just about anything without consequence. This seducing liar would cause the beloved saints to become so comfortable in their lifestyle of mediocrity and lukewarmness that they would dictate to the Most High what they wanted. No longer was the Savior first. No longer were there heard prayers of heart rendering submission and trust. The demon, Complacency, steadily and consistently spread throughout the Kingdom of Light like maple syrup on warm pancakes. It just oozed everywhere, smelling so good, tasting so good, and looking so good, when in fact its paralyzing venom had rendered the

Beloved powerless and ineffective. Complacency whispered, "Everything is fine."

In the meantime, idols were being erected all throughout the Kingdom of God, idols that spoke to the senses and dulled the spirit. The Holy Spirit would gently beckon, "Come here to the Throneroom, and spend time with Father God." The saints would say, "There's a game on. Maybe later." The Holy Spirit would so softly say, "Go, worship with My family Sunday morning". The saints would say, "Ah, busy today." The Holy Spirit would say, "Seek Me first and everything will be added to you." The saints would say, "I've got to work overtime to make ends meet. I don't have time to go to church." The Holy Spirit would weep and say, "Come into the sanctuary and be healed, be ministered to, and trust again." The saints would say, "I've been hurt too many times by the Church. Leave me alone." The Holy Spirit would say, "You see the need, please, help." The saints would say, "I'd rather not get involved." The Bible says meditate on the Word day and night. Pray without ceasing. The saints would say, "Maybe later, I don't have time right now."

Anything or anybody that takes the place or time that God wants becomes an idol before Him and all the while the demon Complacency is celebrating the victory on behalf of the kingdom of darkness. Keep them bound in the "I's" so they won't be controlled by the I AM.

In His Kingdom, God has shed His light upon the deeds of darkness, dispelling the lies and commanding all who are called 'the Beloved' to turn and come and be set free from this demon Complacency. "Rend your heart, not your garment…"

Word of the Lord

"Rend, tear, break your heart for Me.", says the Lord. "Give Me all of you and put Me first again. I do not need your garments; the outside appearance, when your heart is not in My hands. Give Me ALL of who you are and who you want to be. Give Me ALL of your heart. And when you think you've done this give Me ALL your praise, your worship and thanksgiving. And when you have done this, give Me your intimacy, that vulnerable place where no one goes. I want that too. I want your family, your husband, your wife, and your children. And when you've given Me them, give Me your life, your very breath, trusting in Me to give it back to you. And when you have done all this, then REJOICE for I WILL restore the years and everything in those years. The victory will be as great as your willingness to allow Me access to every part of your life. A quick work do I do."

Chapter Six

Restoration of the Shunammite Woman

1 Elisha had told the woman whose son he had brought to life, "Take your family and move to some other country, for the Lord has called down a famine on Israel that will last for seven years."

OBEDIANCE

2 So, the woman took her family and lived in the land of the Philistines for seven years.

3 After the famine ended, she returned to the land of Israel and went to see the king about getting back her house and land.

4 Just as she came in, the king was talking with Gehazi, Elisha's servant, and saying, "Tell me some stories of the great things Elisha has done."

5 And Gehazi was telling the king about the time when Elisha brought a little boy back to life. At that very moment, the mother of the boy walked in! "Oh, sir!"

Gehazi exclaimed, "Here is the woman, now, and this is her son—the very one Elisha brought back to life! "

6 "Is this true?" the king asked her. And she told him that it was. So he directed one of his officials to see to it that everything she had owned was restored to her, plus the value of any crops that had been harvested during her absence. **II Kings 8:1-6** TLB

Strong's Concordance Definition

Restored-7725–To turn back, (hence away), (not necessarily with the idea of return to the starting point); bring again back home draw back, recall, recompense, recover, refresh, relieve, render, (again), repent, requite, rescue, retrieve, reward.

Living in the land of the Philistines meant living in bondage, slavery, and contempt. This Shunammite woman and her family had everything taken from them, including their freedom. They no longer had the finances they were used to. They no longer had the freedom to do, or to be what they were used to doing or being. Their everyday life was turned upside down. For seven years this woman was forced to live in substandard housing, eating what was given to her, when and if it was given to her. Shame was an everyday obstacle now that she had her freedom taken away. She was in the minority. This

Shunammite woman and her family were looked down upon because they were outsiders. Understand she came from a society where godliness and righteousness prevailed. Godly principles, godly ethics were common. She knew no other way of a lifestyle. She was not a prideful woman. She was, however, used to excellence and respect and anything less was foreign to her. To watch her son go through the same was past what she ever thought would be. They were treated like animals. All beauty and humanness was stripped from her. She had a promise though, from the man of God. Elisha told her this ugly existence would only last for seven years. She counted the days, sometimes the hours, to keep the promise alive. This mother also rehearsed the victories, from the past, knowing that if her God could restore her beloved son from the dead, most certainly He could and would restore her home, her values, her livelihood, her grace, honor and the years that were being stolen from her.

She kept her faith in tact, tangible and flexible throughout the tests and trials of drought. The seven years in this kind of living only made her more appreciative of her homeland and what she had. She also grew more intimate with her Husband, Lord Jehovah Jireh, knowing that He would never leave her or forsake her. During the years of bondage, in this dry and foreign land, the Shunammite woman would come to desire a deeper relationship with her Lord. She cherished the times of loneliness because it was there that He would speak to her of days to come where He would restore to her, in abundance, what had been ripped away. Moreover, in those long nights of drought and dryness, she learned who she was, in Him. She learned to receive all that her Lord had for her. This was deposited into her heart, kept in the safe place, so that when the years of drought ended, she would come out into a greater, fuller, more powerful, victorious life. The tears she had shed in the lonely, dry places had not gone unnoticed by her Lord. The psalmist knew her heart when he wrote:

1 When the Lord brought back the captivity of Zion,
we were like those who dream.
2 Then our mouth was filled with
laughter, and our tongue with singing.
Then they said among the nations,
"The Lord has done great things for them."
3 The Lord has done great things for us,
where of we are glad.
4 Bring back our captivity, O Lord,
as the streams of the South.
5 Those who sow in tears
shall reap in joy. **Psalm 126:1-5**

Somehow, someway, her Lord worked a work within her being because when the day came for her to leave the land of captivity, the land of shame and lack, the land of bondage and drought, she knew what to do. In the past, she would have hesitated, questioning her authority and right to claim what was hers. This day, however, she knew who she was, in Him, because during the time of captivity and drought, walls of fear and mistrust (in self) were torn down. The old ways of thinking and seeing herself were ripped out, like old rotten floorboards that were worn from use and misuse. They would be taken up and replaced with new, strong ones thus strengthening the whole structure. She could tell her foundation of faith in her Lord had changed. It was stronger than ever before. She was different.

There was a kick in her step, that day, as she entered the king's palace to reclaim what was rightfully hers. Walking down the long center aisle, leading to the king's throne, this Shunammite woman saw a familiar face, Gehazi, Elisha's faithful servant speaking to the king. To her surprise, she heard her name mentioned and then suddenly, he saw her and yelled so loudly, *"Oh, sir!" Gehazi exclaimed, "Here is the woman now, and this is her son—the very one Elisha brought back to life!"*
II Kings 8:5 TLB

Faith abounded throughout the palace that day as he spoke of the miracle the Lord had performed for this Shunammite woman. The king received her and asked her to expound upon Gehazi's story. As she spoke, all

Opportunity

those years of drought and lack and shame were suddenly taken from her. *"Is this true?" the king asked her. And she told him that it was. So he directed one of his officials to see to it that everything she had owned was restored to her, plus the value of any crops that had been harvested during her absence.* **II Kings 8:6** TLB Right before her eyes, the promise to restore all, was being manifested. She sang and laughed and rejoiced in all that her Lord had done for her and her son.

During her time away, during her time of intimacy and prayer, her Husband was preparing her deliverance. Such a divine appointment! Gehazi was in the king's court at that very hour the Shunammite woman came to ask for her home and land back. At that very hour, they were discussing her!!!

The lifeline of faith had been released into the future during those times of drought, only to manifest the miracle of increase and restoration seven years later!

Chapter Seven

Restoration Perpetuates
Via The Cross

J ust how does God's plan, for restoration, perpetuate itself and become effective? Only through the completed work of the cross, the shed Blood of Jesus Christ, the crucifixion, and resurrection, does restoration begin and at the same time, is fulfilled. How can one event be so complete? In its beginning, the finished work has been accomplished. He, Jesus, is called the Alpha and the Omega, the Beginning and the End. This is why

"Repent, therefore and be converted..." **Acts 3:19** is absolutely vital, and alive, becoming a catalyst to restoration.

19 "Repent therefore and be converted, that your sins may be blotted out, so that times of refreshing may come from the presence of the Lord,

20 and that He may send Jesus Christ, who was preached to you before,

21 whom heaven must receive until the times of <u>*restoration*</u> *of all things, which God has spoken by the mouth of all His holy prophets since the world began."*
Acts 3:19-21

Strong's Concordance Definition

<u>**Restoration/Restitution**</u>–605–(from   600)
Restoration: *a.* of a true theocracy; *b.* of the perfect state before the fall

600 To reconstitute in health, home, or organization; restore again to place down permanently

1 Now Peter and John went up together to the temple at the hour of prayer, the ninth hour.

2 And a certain man <u>*lame from his mother's womb*</u> *was carried, whom they laid daily at the gate of the temple which is called Beautiful, to ask alms from those who entered the temple;*

3 who, seeing Peter and John about to go into the temple, asked for alms.

4 And fixing his eyes on him, with John, Peter said, "Look at us."

5 So he gave them his attention, expecting to receive something from them.

6 Then Peter said, "Silver and gold I do not have, but what I do have I give you: In the name of Jesus Christ of Nazareth, rise up and walk."

7 And he took him by the right hand and lifted him up, and immediately his feet and ankle bones received strength.

8 So he, leaping up, stood and walked and entered the temple with them—walking, leaping, and praising God.

9 And all the people saw him walking and praising God. **Acts 3: 1-9**

Peter and John had just prayed for a man, born crippled, to walk. This man sat daily at the temple gates. Everyone knew him. He was born deformed and ugly. He had no money; he was a beggar by profession because he could not work. The priests and the Sadducees, the religious folk, knew him well because they had to pass him as they went to prayer everyday; however, no one helped him in his deformity. But, listen! Along came Peter and John who had already experienced Acts 3:19, and now they were living in Acts 3:20-21. Restoration was an expected daily reality in and through their lives. They gave what they had to this man and so many others, causing restoration to perpetuate continually. Peter and John repented and were converted. They were living in 'times of refreshing' through the very display of power coming from them when the crippled man, from birth, jumped up and ran all over the place.

Times of Refreshing

'Times of refreshing' was most definitely upon them. 'Times of refreshing' can be translated as revival. They were going to a prayer meeting, and BOOM, revival broke out. Remember the definition of restoration in Strong's Concordance means to reconstitute in health, home, or organization. All the crippled man wanted was money, that's what he expected. However, God had a different plan for this man, his family, and his neighborhood. That day the power of 'times of refreshing' came upon the crippled man from birth, bringing restoration of health, of home and of organization. His whole life, his neighborhood, and his family would change now that he was made whole, restored. All his neighbors heard what happened to him. *All the people saw him walking and praising God and they knew that it was he who sat begging alms at the Beautiful Gate of the temple; and they were filled with wonder and amazement at what had happened to him.* **Acts 3:9-10** The people from all around, who knew him as a deformed, crippled beggar, came as they heard from those who saw the two men perform a miracle. Peter reminded them that they did nothing to this man, but rather it was them who *"...denied the Holy One and the Just......and killed the Prince of Life, whom God raised from the dead..."* **Acts 3:14-15** Peter went on to boldly proclaim in **Acts 3:16** *"And His name, through* *faith in His name, has made this man strong, whom you see and know. Yes, the faith which comes through Him has given him this perfect soundness in the presence of you all."* When Peter finished his preaching, 'times of refreshing' spilled out on five thousand people! Even the Sanhedrin acknowledged the miracle. They did everything they could to arrest Peter and John that day, however **Acts 4:14,16** says, *And seeing the man who had been healed standing with them, they could say nothing against it. "…what shall we do to these men? For, indeed, a notable miracle has been done through them is evident to all who dwell in Jerusalem, and we cannot deny it."* ALL of Jerusalem heard what happened that day! Five thousand were converted! Five thousand people did what Peter and John preached, out of their own 'times of refreshing'. As Peter and John experienced revival and restoration, five thousand men repented and were converted. Their sins were blotted out and times of refreshing came upon THEM!

Restoration was given a place to live, to perpetuate and to grow in five thousand men as they brought salvation home to their families, their neighborhoods, their work places and organizations. The lifeblood of Jesus made a permanent change that day in the lives of thousands with a 'trickle-down' affect on humanity throughout the ages to come.

Chapter Eight

Restoration Scriptures and Prayers

1 *Then Elisha spoke to the woman whose son he had restored to life...* **II Kings 8:1**

Restored -2421–To live, have life, remain alive, sustain life, live prosperously, live forever, be quickened, be alive, be restored to life or health

6 And when the king asked the woman, she told him. So the king appointed a certain officer for her, saying, "Restore (7725) *all that was hers, and all the proceeds of the field from the day that she left the land until now."* **II Kings 8:6**

10 And the Lord restored (7725) *Job's losses when he prayed for his friends. Indeed the Lord gave Job twice as much as he had before.* **Job 42:10**

7 The law of the Lord is perfect, <u>restoring</u> (7725) the whole person; **Psalm 19:7**

3 He <u>restores</u> (7725) my soul… **Psalm 23:3**

12 <u>Restore</u> (7725) to me the joy of Your salvation, and uphold me with Your generous Spirit **Psalm 51:12**

26 "I will <u>restore</u> (7725) your judges as at the first, and your counselors as at the beginning. Afterward you shall be called the city of righteousness, the faithful city." **Isaiah 1:26**

Restore–7725–To turn back (hence, away) (not necessarily with the idea of return to the starting point); bring back home draw back, recall, recompense, recover, refresh, relieve render (again) repent, requite, rescue, retrieve, reward

✱ *31 Yet when he (the thief) is found, he must <u>restore</u> (7999) sevenfold; he may have to give up all the substance of his house.* **Proverb 6:31**

25 "So I will <u>restore</u> (7999) to you the years that the swarming locust has eaten, the crawling locust, the consuming locust and the chewing locust…" **Joel 2:25**

25 And I will <u>restore</u> (7999) or replace for you the years that the locust has eaten—the hopping locust, the stripping locust, and the crawling locust, My great army which I sent among you.

26 And you shall eat in plenty and be satisfied and praise the name of the Lord, your God, Who has dealt wondrously with you. And My people shall never be put to shame.

27 And you shall know, understand and realize that I am in the midst of Israel and that I the Lord am your God and there is none else. My people shall never be put to shame. **Joel 2:25-27** AMP

<u>Restore–</u>7999–To be in a covenant of peace; to be safe (in mind, body, or estate); to be completed; to reciprocate; make amends; make an end, finish, full, give again, make good, repay, make to be at peace, make prosperous, requite, make restitution, reward, by impl. to be friendly

17 'For I will <u>restore</u> (5927) health to you and heal you of your wounds,' says the Lord, 'Because they called you an outcast saying: "This is Zion; no one seeks her."' **Jeremiah 30:17**

18 I have seen his ways, and heal him; I will also lead him, and <u>restore</u> (5927) comforts to him and to his mourners. **Isaiah 57:18**

12 Return to the strongholds, you prisoners of hope. Even today I declare that I will <u>restore</u> (5927) double to you. **Zechariah 9:12**

1 For behold, in those days and at that time when I shall reverse the captivity and <u>restore</u> (5927) the fortunes of Judah and Jerusalem… **Joel 3:1** AMP

<u>Restore</u>–5927–to ascend, arise (up), (cause to) ascend up, at once, break (the day) (up), bring (up), (cause to) burn, carry up, increase, lay, leap, levy, lift (self) up, light, make to pay, raise, recover, shoot forth (up), (begin to) spring (up), stir up.

5 Also let the gold and silver articles of the house of God, which Nebuchadnezzar took from the temple which is in Jerusalem and brought to Babylon, be <u>restored</u> (8421) and taken back to the temple which is in Jerusalem, each to its place; and deposit them in the house of God. **Ezra 6:5**

<u>Restored</u>–8421–To come back

5 So when He had looked around at them with anger, being grieved by the hardness of their hearts, He said to the man, "Stretch out your hand." And he stretched it out, and his hand was <u>restored</u> (600) as whole as the other. (hand was withered) **Mark 3:5**

25 Then He put His hands on his eyes again and made him look up. And he was <u>restored</u> (600) and saw everyone clearly. **Mark 8:25**

<u>Restored</u>–600–To reconstitute in health, home or organization; to restore to its former state

19 "Repent therefore and be converted, that your sins may be blotted out, so that times of refreshing may come from the presence of the Lord,

20 "and that He may send Jesus Christ, who was preached to you before,

21 "whom heaven must receive until the times of <u>restoration</u> (605) of all things, which God has spoken by the mouth of all His holy prophets since the world began." **Acts 3:19-21**

...until the times of <u>restitution</u> (605) of all things... **Acts 3:21 KJV**

11 And if the Spirit of Him Who raised up Jesus from the dead dwells in you, then He Who raised up Christ Jesus from the dead will also <u>restore</u> (605) to life your mortal short-lived, perishable bodies through His Spirit Who dwells in you. **Romans 8:11** AMP

<u>Restitution/Restoration</u>–605 from 600–To reconstitute in health, home, or organization; restore again to place down permanently; restoration: a. of a true theocracy; b. of the perfect state before the fall

Prayers
Prayer of Recommitment

Father, I come boldly to Your throne of grace in time of need and ask You to forgive me for not keeping You first in my life. Father, I repent for having idols before You. I repent Lord for being lukewarm and complacent in my walk with You. I repent Lord for any sin of unforgiveness that I may have toward my brothers and sisters in the Lord. I repent for not keeping unity within the Body of Christ. I repent Lord for putting my agenda before Yours. I bring my life before You and I ask You to wash me from all unrighteousness and self-centeredness. Wash me with the Blood of Jesus and restore to me a steadfast spirit to serve You 100%. Heal me I pray, and restore my soul, in Jesus' name.

Prayer to Restore Joy

Father, in these days ahead I ask You to send times of refreshing so that the joy of my salvation is restored. Lord, I purpose to seek You with all my heart. I make You Lord over every part of my life again as I submit to You. I receive Your love to me and Your grace and the power of Your Holy Spirit to do what I have been created to do for You. Thank You Father, in Jesus' name. Amen

Prayer for the Solomon Kind of Wisdom

Father, I come to You in the name of Jesus and ask for Your wisdom to do what I have been called to do as a part of Your Living Temple. Solomon knew he could not be king and rule effectively without Your wisdom, so he asked for it and You gave him specific wisdom for the task at hand. Father, I may not have been called to be king, however, I believe I have been called do this,_____ so I ask for specific wisdom in accomplishing the plan You have for me which is, _____ so I will be as successful as Solomon was. I purpose to set time aside to fellowship with You and listen to Your voice. I give You all the acknowledgement and glory.

Thank You Lord, in Jesus' name. Amen.

Building the Temple of God Scriptures and Prayer

20 But you, beloved, building yourselves up on your most holy faith, praying in the Holy Spirit, **Jude vs. 20**

6 As you have therefore received Christ Jesus the Lord, so walk in Him,

7 rooted and built up in Him and established in the faith, as you have been taught, abounding in it with thanksgiving. **Colossians 2:6-7**

21 in whom the whole building, being joined together, grows into a holy temple in the Lord,
22 in whom you also are being built together for a habitation of God in the Spirit. **Ephesians 2:21-22**

16 Do you not know that you are the temple of God and that the Spirit of God dwells in you? **I Corinthians 3:16**

Scripture Proclamation

I am constantly building myself up in my most holy faith, praying in the Spirit and I walk in Him, rooted and built up in Him and established in faith. I am joined together with the Body of Christ, in unity, as we all grow into a holy temple in the Lord.

Prayer to Receive Jesus Christ as Savior and Lord

Father God, I come before You right now. I ask You to forgive me for the not believing in You. I ask You to forgive me for any sin in my life, I renounce all involvement that I may have had in the occult and I say with my mouth and believe in my heart that Jesus Christ is the

Son of God and I receive You, Jesus as my Savior and my Lord. Old things are now passed away and behold, all things are brand new. I am a new creation in Christ. Thank You for saving me. I ask that Your the Holy Spirit fill me, now, with His power.

I will serve You, Lord the rest of my life.

In Jesus' name,

Amen.

Conclusion

It's Restoration Time, Beloved

⚜

G od-inspired restoration cannot be reversed. He
promised *'times of restoration of ALL things'* Acts
3:21. Have we seen this on planet earth? Has it happened
yet? No, not to the fullest, however, the shed Blood of
Jesus Christ has set the provision in place. Are we in the
'time'? We are the Church as spoken of in the book of
Acts. Peter preached of a day to come when 'all things'
will be restored. To whom? To the Church. When? Acts
3:20 speaks of the second return of Jesus. That is the end
times. We are in the end times, now! ALL things must
be restored back to His Church before His great and
glorious return. Now, that is good news! The promise of
God in **Joel 2:25** *"So I will restore to you the years that
the swarming locust has eaten, the crawling locust, the
consuming locust, and the chewing locust…"* has been
prophesied and proclaimed.

Bring back, to the Living Temple, O Lord, that which was common during the days of Solomon's reign, in the temple made of stone; Your Shekinah presence.

Restore Your beauty, Your covenant, Your wealth, Your joy, Your unity, Your worship, Your wisdom, Your government.

O God, restore as of old, Your glory, so that as unbelievers pass by Your Living Temple, they would weaken and submit to You.

IT'S RESTORATION TIME!!!

Family love + unity
Self worth /Value
Expression/ Acceptance
An earthly father
My mother's affection
Education
Travel
Health
Self-control
Still born
Covenant/marriage
Opportunity
Home
~~Pleasure~~
Peace
Wealth
Soundness of mind

CPSIA information can be obtained at www.ICGtesting.com
Printed in the USA
BVOW02s2058100715

408185BV00001B/42/P